The Very Boastful Kangaroo

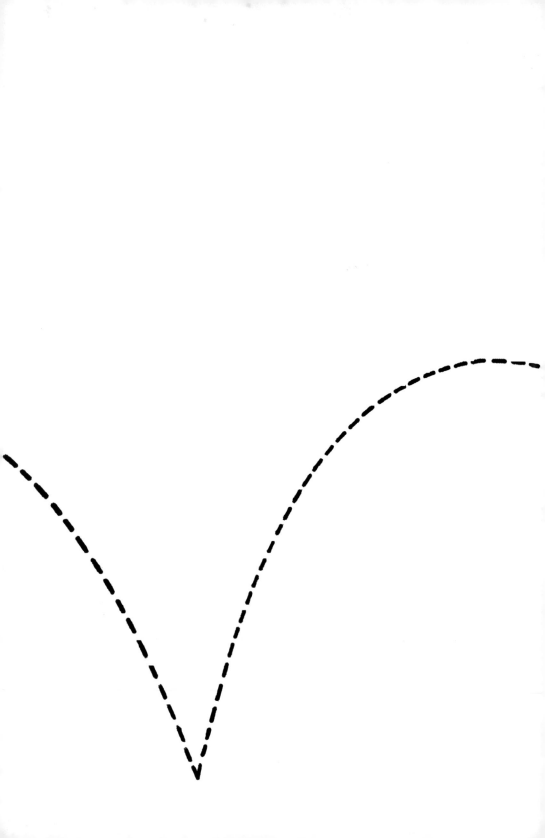

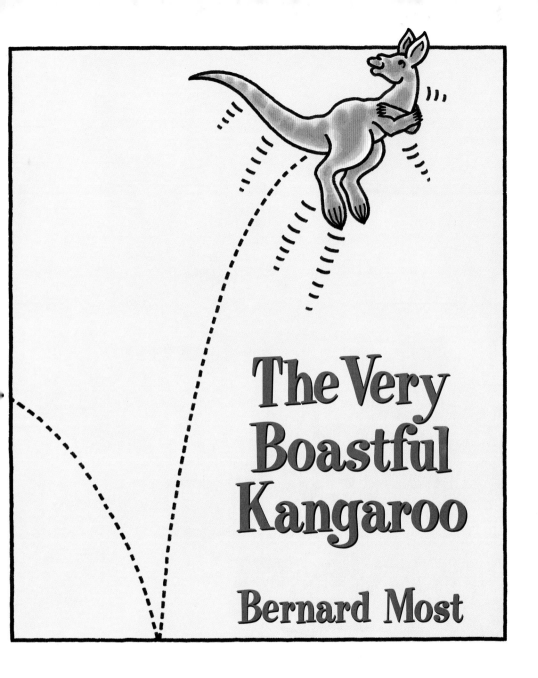

The Very Boastful Kangaroo

Bernard Most

Green Light Readers
Harcourt, Inc.
San Diego   New York   London

First Green Light Readers edition 1999
Green Light Readers is a registered trademark of Harcourt, Inc.

Library of Congress Cataloging-in-Publication Data
Most, Bernard.
The very boastful kangaroo/Bernard Most.
p. cm.—(Green Light Readers)
Summary: A very, very boastful kangaroo brags that it can jump higher than
anyone, but a teeny, tiny kangaroo cleverly wins the jumping contest.
[1. Kangaroos—Fiction. 2. Contests—Fiction.] I. Title. II. Series.
PZ7.M8544Ve 1999
[E]—dc21 98-55234
ISBN 0-15-202349-6
ISBN 0-15-202266-X (pb)
Printed in Mexico
B D F H J K I G E C
A C E G I J H F D B (pb)

This story is about a very, very boastful kangaroo.

"I can jump so, so high!" he bragged.

"No one can jump higher than I can!"

Just then a little kangaroo jumped up. "Let's have a jumping contest," she said. "Can you jump higher than these kangaroos can?"

"Oh yes," said the very, very boastful kangaroo. "I can jump much, much higher than any kangaroo! I'll win the contest because I'm the best!"

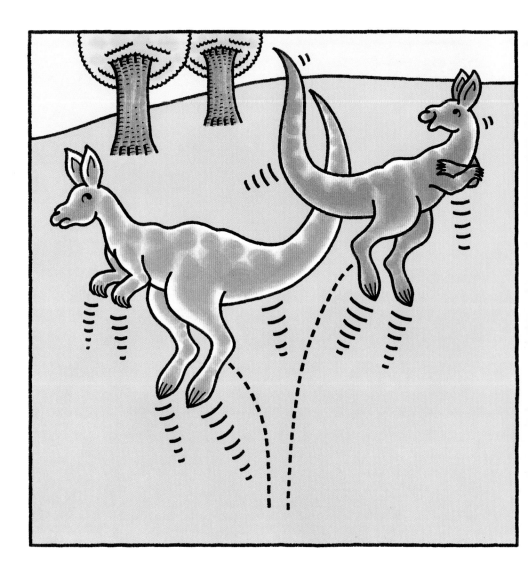

The first kangaroo jumped high. The very, very boastful kangaroo jumped even higher.

"See?" bragged the very, very boastful kangaroo. "I can jump higher. I'm the best!"

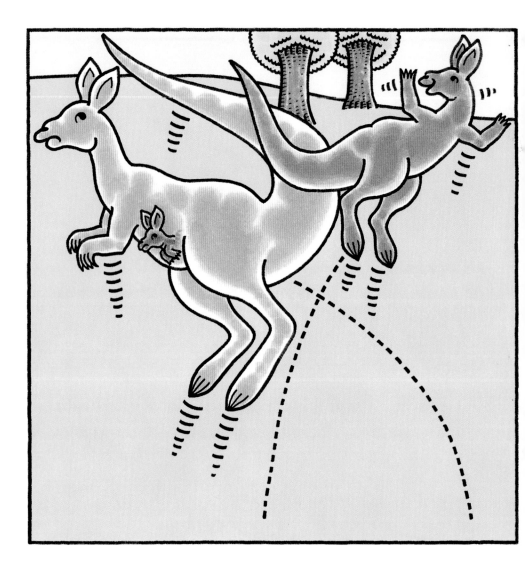

The next kangaroo jumped very high.
Even so, the very, very boastful
kangaroo jumped much higher.

"See?" the very, very boastful kangaroo bragged. "I win! I win the jumping contest."

"Not yet!" yelled a teeny, tiny kangaroo. "Can you jump higher than that tall tree?"

"That tree is much, much too tall!" said the very, very boastful kangaroo. "Even I can't jump higher than that tree!"

"If I jump higher than that tree, do I win the contest?" asked the teeny, tiny kangaroo.

The very, very boastful kangaroo giggled. "Yes, but you're not going to do it."

The teeny, tiny kangaroo jumped a
teeny, tiny jump. Then she shouted,
"I win! I win the contest …
BECAUSE TREES CAN'T JUMP!"

All the kangaroos giggled and giggled—even the very, very boastful kangaroo!

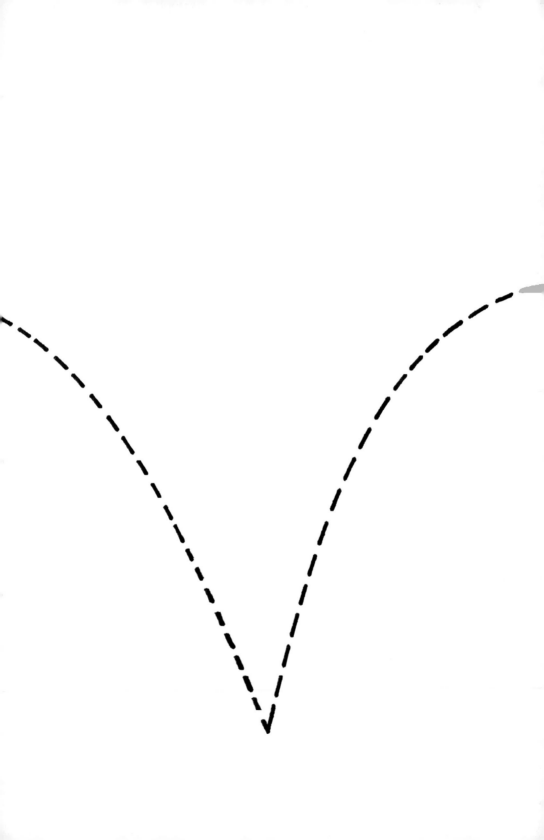

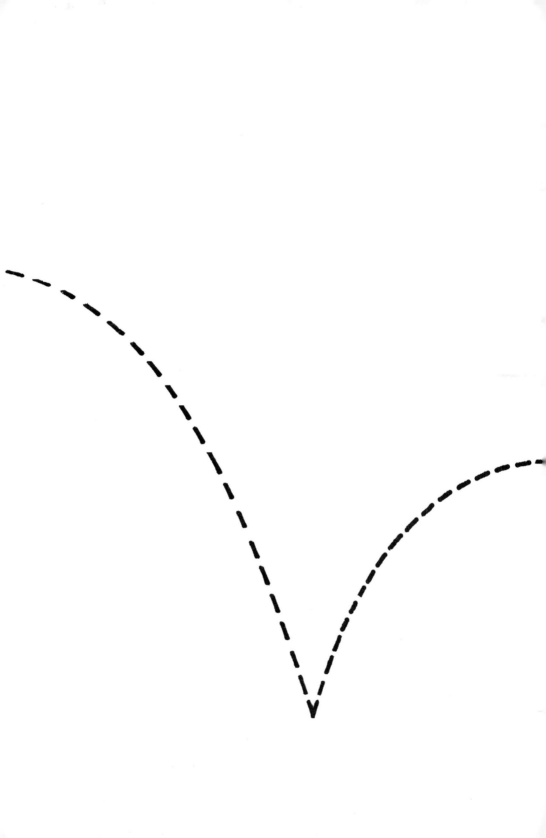

Meet the Author-Illustrator

Bernard Most likes his characters to find interesting ways to solve problems. In **The Very Boastful Kangaroo**, the teeny, tiny kangaroo finds a smart way to win the jumping contest. The author-illustrator wants his readers to know that even though they are small, they can do anything they want if they just try. Mr. Most always tells children to follow their dreams and to "never give up!"

Walt Chrynwski

Bernard Most